Spook Night

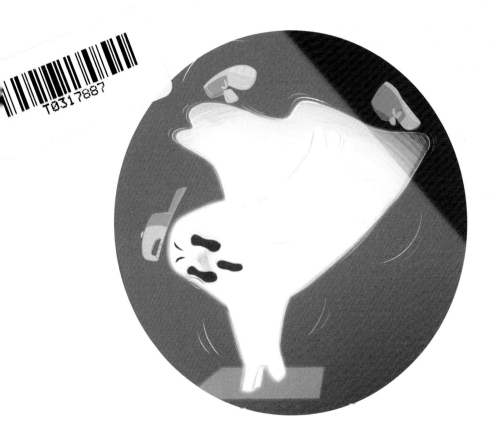

Written by Samantha Montgomerie

Illustrated by Elena Napoli

Collins

On Spook Night, do not go to sleep. You must spot the spooks on Starlight Street.

As the darkness starts to come,
owls swoop down to join the fun.

Drac spins the monster disc.
The song booms and fingers
start to click.

Frank joins in, all in green.
He creeps to the spotlight to be seen.

Creeper starts to flutter and float.
He bops with Boo in her sparkling coat.

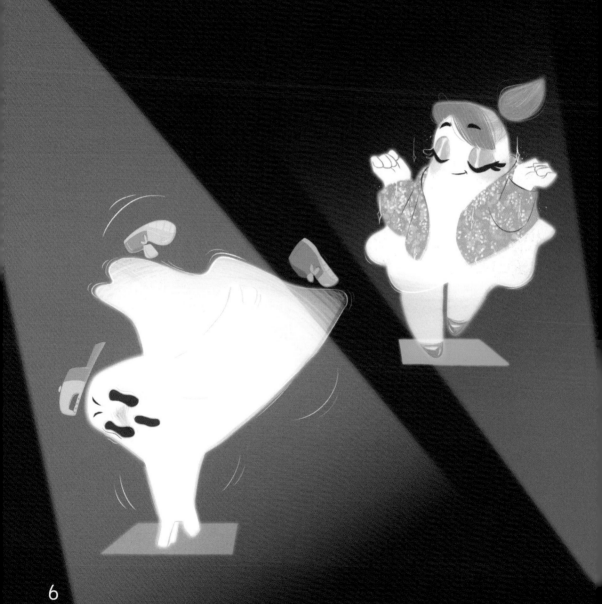

Crook joins in, rattling along,
clicking and clacking to
the booming song.

Screech and Swoop flap up with glee.
They zoom and flutter to the tree.

Hoo swoops up to the red balloons.
She hoots and flaps into the gloom.

Howler hops with Spooker and Fright.
He snarls "Yahoo!" in the flashing light.

Fang joins in, sweeping along.
He starts to kick to the booming song.

On Spook Night, do not go to sleep.
Meet a spook on Starlight Street.

Join them in the flashing lights,
for monster songs and fun all night.

Spook Night

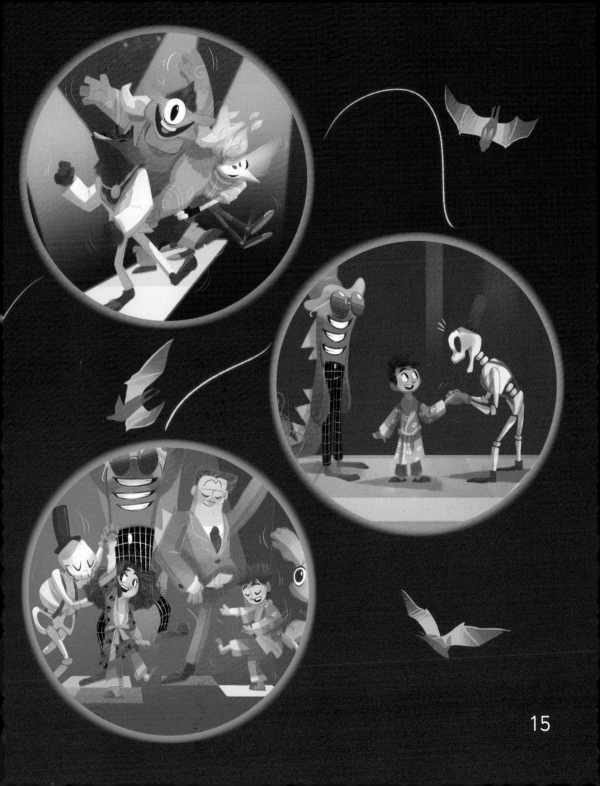

 After reading

Letters and Sounds: Phase 4

Word count: 165

Focus on adjacent consonants with long vowel phonemes, e.g. *green*.

Common exception words: do, you, go, to, the, come, all, he, be, they, have, she, into

Curriculum links: Music: Use their voices expressively and creatively by singing songs and speaking chants and rhymes

National Curriculum learning objectives: Reading/word reading: apply phonic knowledge and skills as the route to decode words; read accurately by blending sounds in unfamiliar words containing GPCs that have been taught; Reading/comprehension: understand both the books they can already read accurately and fluently and those they listen to by making inferences on the basis of what is being said and done

Developing fluency

- Read the book together with your child, enjoying the rhythm and noticing the rhyming words.
- You could take turns to read a page.

Phonic practice

- Encourage your child to practise reading words that contain adjacent consonants with long vowels.
  - Turn to page 6 and point to **Creeper**. Ask your child to sound out and blend. (C/r/ee/p/er)
  - Repeat for: page 3 **swoop** (s/w/oo/p); page 10 **snarls** (s/n/ar/l/s); page 12 **Starlight** (S/t/ar/l/igh/t)

Extending vocabulary

- Focus on the character names. Ask your child to think about each name, look at the pictures and suggest alternative spooky names for their favourites, e.g.

  Drac (*Sucker, Vamp*)   Crook (*Rattler, Bones*)   Howler (*Wolf, Hairy-Scary*)   Fang (*Web, Biter*)

Comprehension

- Turn to pages 14 and 15 and ask your child to imagine they are one of the children at Spook Night. Ask them to describe the spooky characters and what they do, using the pictures as prompts.